D0630410

FIREWALL

FIREWALL

Sean Rodman

orca soundings

ORCA BOOK PUBLISHERS

Library and Archives Canada Cataloguing in Publication

Rodman, Sean, 1972-,
Firewall / Sean Rodman.
(Orca soundings)

Issued in print and electronic formats.
ISBN 978-1-4598-1453-0 (softcover).—ISBN 978-1-4598-1454-7 (pdf).—
ISBN 978-1-4598-1455-4 (epub)

I. Title. II. Series: Orca soundings
PS8635.O355F57 2017   jc813'.6   C2017-900833-1
C2017-900834-X

First published in the United States, 2017
Library of Congress Control Number: 2017933024

Summary: In this high-interest novel for teen readers, Josh discovers
a virtual town that is eerily similar to his own.

*Orca Book Publishers is dedicated to preserving the environment and has
printed this book on Forest Stewardship Council® certified paper.*

Orca Book Publishers gratefully acknowledges the support for its
publishing programs provided by the following agencies: the Government
of Canada through the Canada Book Fund and the Canada Council
for the Arts, and the Province of British Columbia through
the BC Arts Council and the Book Publishing Tax Credit.

Edited by Tanya Trafford
Cover image by Dreamstime.com

ORCA BOOK PUBLISHERS
www.orcabook.com

Printed and bound in Canada.

20 19 18 17 • 4 3 2 1

To my family, who support my writing habit with passion and patience. I couldn't do it without you.

Chapter One

I'm made of high-caliber awesome.

Check me out. I'm the hulking guy dressed in combat gear, lurking in the shadows of a bombed-out building. My blue-uniformed torso is draped in ammunition, a one-man arsenal. And the gun I'm holding—there's no way on earth that anyone could realistically grip this massive multi-barreled weapon of destruction.

But I can. Because—like I said—high-caliber awesome.

All right, full disclosure. Obviously, that's not actually me. In real life, chicken-bone arms stick out from my faded black T-shirt. I have puff-ball brown hair and a spattering of zits around my nose. I'm a little short, just enough that I never get picked for basketball. That combined with my baby face makes everyone think I'm in ninth grade—even though I'm in eleventh. Not too surprisingly, I prefer the on-screen version of myself. It's part of the reason why *Killswitch* is my favorite video game. In the game, I'm a "war-fighter." A cyborg warrior. Here in the real world, I'm a gamer. And a nerd.

I find the can of Monster Juice next to my keyboard and take a swig. Readjusting my headset so the microphone is closer to my lips, I wipe each sweaty hand on my jeans before grasping the controller again. I make my warfighter turn in a circle, surveying our bombed-out headquarters.

"Griggs?" I say into the microphone. "You logged in?"

"Keep your diaper on, Josh." His voice fuzzes out from my headset. "My connection sucks, and I'm a little laggy tonight. Let me try again." A few seconds later, another warfighter appears next to me on the screen. Identical blue super-soldier armor, except for a glowing green "tag" floating above his head. That shows that this soldier is on my side.

"I'm in," Griggs says. "You see me now?" His guy moves a little jerkily, stuttering in little pixelated jumps as he turns around.

"Yep," I answer. "All right, let's go. First stop is the helipad."

Both warfighters start jogging smoothly out of the ruined building, and the view opens up. It's a battlefield, the scene of a war in progress. A war that won't end as long as we keep playing. The camera tracking our two characters follows us down into a crater. Griggs stops and covers me while I inch forward carefully. I peer over the far edge of the crater. Tracer fire in the distance arcs between two broken-down skyscrapers. I hear a rushing sound in my headset and flatten to the ground. Just in time, too, as something huge swoops by overhead. It looks like the evil love child of a military helicopter and a dragonfly—a bugchopper. The roar in my headset is deafening. I tap on the keyboard to drop the volume down.

"You got that one?" I say. Turning around, I see Griggs is already aiming his massive weapon at the bugchopper as it soars away. There's a flash of yellow light that obscures the screen. The missile quickly closes in on the helicopter, trailing jagged clouds of exhaust. There is a second flash of light as the target disintegrates.

"Yes!" says Griggs. "Suck it!" The tag above his warfighter flashes as he racks up some extra points. His super-soldier does some weird little jerky moves—Griggs's victory dance, I guess.

"Yeah, yeah. You're the big man," I say. "Just watch my back, okay?" I push my controller forward and clamber over the side of the crater. Gun up, crosshairs floating midair, ready for anything.

Almost. I've walked right into an ambush—a group of soldiers is waiting for us. Warfighters just like Griggs and me, except their armor is red. Other players sitting in their bedrooms some-where, ready to atomize us. I key the button on my controller to bring up my flamethrower. Pulsing red crosshairs appear, floating over an enemy soldier's helmet. A clean head shot. The flame-thrower will be overkill. Satisfying though.

Before I can squeeze the trigger, my world dissolves into jittery static, filled with bullets and laser fire. Messages in tiny script start scrolling up from the bottom of my screen—[low health, critical hit.] My warfighter jerks randomly and stumbles backward. The screen is so full of gunfire that I can't even see the guys who are killing me. This isn't right. They shouldn't be able to deliver that much heat. Whoever this is, they're cheating somehow.

Dimly I hear a muffled hammering sound. I ignore it and keep jamming the buttons on my controller.

"Griggs!" I call out. "What the hell is going on?" Stabbing the controller buttons, I slowly manage to turn my

character around. It's not dignified—
I'm running away in slow motion. As I
inch forward, I see Griggs's warfighter
lying on the ground. There's a red X
floating over the body. He's toast. Dead.
His voice crackles through my headset.

"Sorry, man. I think they got me
with a grenade." I flinch at the crunch
of an explosion on-screen and watch
my warfighter suddenly fly through the
air. He lands in a crumpled heap on the
ground. I'm tagged with a red hovering
X as well.

"Dammit," I mutter. I was pretty
proud of my warfighter. Spent way too
much time grinding through levels,
loading up on weapons and armor. And
now he's dead—I'm dead. Just like that.
On-screen, a group of soldiers dressed
in red combat armor jerkily run around
our bodies, scooping up gear and ammunition. Then they disappear out of sight,
leaving my digital corpse behind.

"Who were those guys?" I ask Griggs.

"Wolf Clan, I think," says Griggs. "There was something sketchy going on there. Think they had cheat codes?" I can hear the disappointment in his voice too. "Want to respawn? One more game?"

The muffled hammering is back. Louder. More insistent. I realize it's not a sound effect from the game and pull the headset down from around my ears. It's my dad, banging on the bedroom door.

"Joshua? Open the door. Right now." My dad is a cop, and he's using his command-and-control voice. The one that makes perps drop their guns and piss their pants. I've built up an immunity to it. Mostly. I slap the laptop lid closed. Pull out a random binder from my backpack and flip it open, hiding the laptop beneath it. Then I open the door.

Dad's in his pyjamas, which does nothing to make him seem more cuddly. A broken nose that never set right sticks out from his round, jowly face. His friends on the force call him "Big Dog," and it's an appropriate nickname. Bark, bite—both are unpleasant.

"You know what time it is?" he says. Gray eyes bore steadily into mine. I make a show of looking around for a clock.

"I don't know, but it's really late. Thing is, I've got this math test tomorrow, and I don't want to screw it up. Still trying to get used to the new textbook. It's all different from my old school." Dad still feels guilty about the divorce. About moving us away from big-city Chicago to rural little Valleytown, two time zones away from everything and everyone that I grew up with.

I play the guilt card whenever I can. But he's not buying it tonight.

"Don't give me that bull. I heard you shouting to your buddies, playing that damn game. You think I'm deaf and blind?" He stomps into the room, filling the doorframe and crowding me out of the way. He looks down at the open math binder and flips through a few lined pages. "This looks pretty blank to me." He nudges it aside, revealing the laptop. Dad lays a big meaty palm on it for a moment.

"Your computer feels pretty warm, like it's been running for a couple of hours." It sucks having a cop for a dad. "I'll hold on to this for a while."

"No, c'mon. That's not fair," I say. It sounds like begging—it is begging—and I wince. He hates that. Dad's face toughens up even further. He tucks the silver laptop under his arm and turns toward the door.

"Mom wouldn't do this to me," I say. I snap the words out like tracer rounds, and they stop Dad cold. He half-turns back to me, his bald head shaking slowly back and forth. He grimaces like he's swallowing something he doesn't like.

"Get to sleep. We'll talk about this tomorrow." He turns away and doesn't look back, just turns out the light and clicks the door shut.

I flop back onto my bed. Pulling my phone out of my pocket, I text Griggs.

Busted. AWK for tonight. Away from keyboard. Maybe permanently. I flip through the incoming texts on my phone. A couple from Jane, back in Chicago. That's complicated. I can't handle texting her back right now. Not that I ever can. It's been weeks.

So I shut the phone down and lie there in the dark.

I can imagine a bright red X hovering over my body, just like in the game. I'm dead in the virtual world, and my real life sucks even more.

Chapter Two

"Pod people."

Griggs looks at me sideways, twisting the hood of his black rain jacket. "Say what?"

"I said *pod people*. That's what they are." I nod at the clumps of students gathered outside McCallum High. "They're like some kind of alien species.

All identical. And if you get too close…"
I mime my brain being sucked out of my head.

"What, you become one of the pod people?" says Griggs.

"Exactly."

We study the students milling about in the parking lot. The school day complete, hundreds of them now shuffle through. Waiting under cold autumn skies to be evacuated from the school grounds by a fleet of yellow buses. On the brick wall beside us, someone has scrawled a meaningless graffiti tag in black balloon letters— **SUDO**. I shiver as a gust of wind blows through the crowd and cuts right into my thin jacket.

"I beg to differ," says Griggs. "Well, maybe you're right about the brain-sucking thing. I don't know. But they aren't all the same."

I check my phone. Another ten minutes before the bus will arrive. Another text from Jane, wondering why I haven't replied to her. "All right, enlighten me."

I watch Griggs, holding his arms across his body for warmth, rotate like a radar dish until he's pointing at a gaggle of girls. They all hold pastel-colored umbrellas. They all have long hair, varying only in the shades of brown and blond.

"Those are the socialites, also known as the girly-girls." He continues to rotate slowly, naming groups as he goes.

"Drama kids." Dressed mostly in black. A lot of loud laughing.

"Skaters." Three guys, big plaid jackets and ballcaps. Skateboards strapped to their backpacks.

"Wangsters." Griggs is looking outside of the corral where we're all waiting for the buses. Out there, in a second parking lot, stands a group of guys clustered around a new Honda Civic. It's pimped out with neon, spoilers and chrome.

"What's a wangster?" I ask.

"Wannabe gangsters. They like the bling-bling. And would survive about five seconds in a real 'hood."

"True dat, homie," I say.

"Don't ever say that again," says Griggs. "Don't be a wangster."

I laugh. "So which group are you part of?"

Griggs pushes back the hood of his jacket, releasing his staticky hair into the air. "Well, see, this is where you're really wrong about the pod-people thing." With a diesel grunt, our bus comes around the corner and slides into the space in front of us. We line up, the crowd congealing into order.

"What do you mean?" I say.

"You said before that if you get too close, the pod people make you one of their own?"

"Yeah?"

"Truth is, nobody wants guys like us in their group. We will not be assimilated by the pod."

We climb up into the bus, the over-heated air inside filled with its distinctive odors of vinyl and sweat.

"Yeah, fine. Who would want to be?" I say. I find a free seat and slide in, leaving room for Griggs beside me. We shove our backpacks down below the seat.

"You say that—and I get your rebel, I'm-a-loner-new-kid thing." Griggs pulls a can of Monster Juice from the side of his pack and snaps it open. "But I bet you had a pod back in Chicago."

I think about that for a moment. I had Jane—best friend, kind-of girlfriend.

One or two other gamer buddies, people I'd known since forever. Not much of a pod. It's a thousand miles away anyway.

Griggs gives up waiting for me to say something. "Whatever. I don't have a specific pod either. But here's what I've figured out. Each of those groups? They can't interact. If the skaters want something from the socialites? Ain't gonna happen. Invisible wall. Worlds apart." He takes a swig from his can. He nods at a boy in goth makeup as he files down the aisle past us. The goth half-smiles in return.

"So this whole…ecosystem…needs a few free agents," Griggs continues. "People that aren't part of any group but are tolerated by everybody. That's me."

"You're…tolerated?"

"I'm mildly acceptable to all." Griggs finishes his drink, raising it in a toast. "I'm a man of the people."

"Yo, G," says someone behind us. We turn around. He's big—like, football-player big—and squished into the bus seat. "You got another Monster?"

"Sorry, man, last one," says Griggs. The big kid grunts. Shrugs. Slides his headphones back onto his bald head, eyes closing.

"So what category does your friend back there fit into?" I ask. "Jock? Meathead?"

Griggs's brow furrows. "Dude, you don't talk like that in front of—"

A heavy hand lands on my shoulder. "I miss something?" I look back to see Meathead's face inches away from mine. His headphones are still on, but he can clearly hear me just fine.

"I was just asking Griggs," I say carefully, "what to call you." Where did this go off the rails?

"Josh," says Griggs in a warning tone.

"I can think of a couple names for you," says Meathead in a low voice.

"I think we got off on the wrong foot here, gentlemen," interrupts Griggs. "Josh, meet Aaron Carnavon, star linebacker for Valleytown Vikings. Ripped his knee up and is now off the field for a bit while he does rehab. No sports, and he can't drive his sweet ride. Makes him a little irritable."

Meathead/Aaron keeps staring at me. Griggs continues on.

"Aaron, meet Josh. Newly arrived from Chicago. Still figuring things out. Clearly."

Aaron gives me one last hard look, then slumps back into his seat and closes his eyes. I can hear the tinny sound as he cranks up the volume on his tunes.

"You are a world-class idiot," Griggs says, leaning over to whisper. "That guy can hunt you down and stomp you with only one good leg. And what did he do to you?"

"What's his problem? We were just talking," I say. "Look, I get it. I don't fit in here. I'm okay with going it alone. Why aren't you?"

Griggs shakes his head. "You just don't understand. Dude, high school is a combat zone. You won't survive it solo. Someone has to watch your back."

"And that's you?" I say, raising an eyebrow. "You're my big tough bodyguard?"

"For now," says Griggs.

"Why?"

"I find you mildly acceptable."

"Shut up," I say, punching him in the shoulder. But we're both smiling again.

Chapter Three

When I get home, there's good news in the form of a note from my dad on the kitchen table. A yellow sticky note with his scrawl on it, stuck to my laptop: *Working evening shift. Use this for homework only. Dad.*

And honestly, I try to be good. Make myself some mac and cheese, but with a side of vegetables. Clean up all the dishes.

Do my math and socials homework. Lock up the house. Then go to bed by ten.

I try. I really do.

But just as I'm drifting off, my phone buzzes with an incoming text. Jane.

Why won't u call?

Now I'm wide awake again. I spend thirty minutes lying there with my eyes open, staring at the streetlight through my window. I don't have an answer for her. And it's clear that sleep isn't going to happen for a while yet. I quietly reach over and snag my laptop off the desk. Flipping it on, I log back into *Killswitch*. The company logo appears first, intertwined letters in gothic script. Then the menu screen. A message pops up in a chat box in the corner of the screen.

[GRIGGS: back online?]

[JOSH: totally. better stick to text, skip the headsets. don't want Big Dog to hear me and lose laptop again.] I type quietly. I might be paranoid, but if Dad shows up unexpectedly and finds me gaming? Not good. Best to be stealthy.

Griggs sends me a bunch of laughing cartoon-face emoticons, then:

[GRIGGS: which mod?]

[JOSH: not wolf clan. they were sketchy. not sure what. hold on.]

I click through different matches currently in progress. Thing is, since *Killswitch* became really popular, there are more and more idiots playing. Like those guys who killed my character. Groups who form a team or "clan," buy a bunch of upgrades and go on a rampage. They don't actually try to play the game the way it was designed. It was supposed to be about stealth and smarts. If you play it right, *Killswitch* is all about building up your defenses, sneaking around enemy bases, creating new weapons. Using your brain to outwit the guards. Stuff that I'm good at.

That leaves playing the "mods." The game designers of *Killswitch* decided to include a construction kit with the game, allowing anybody to modify the game to create their own version to play. It's like playing with building blocks. Only you end up creating a virtual world where other people can join in. Some people get right into designing them— there are hundreds of mods available on the server. I scroll through the listings. Most of them have stupid names like *JAYIZAWESOME* and are equally lame.

But it's late, and I'm bored. There has to be something worth playing. Then I find one I haven't seen before. *VTON*. I message Griggs, then click on the title. A couple of seconds to load up, and I'm in. Griggs's soldier appears next to me in a showy burst of gold static. I slowly pan around, taking in the landscape around us.

It's nothing like any of the games I've ever played in *Killswitch*. Or anywhere, come to think of it.

[GRIGGS: ????] Griggs is clearly as confused as I am.

There are no ruined buildings, no battlefield, no hovering bugchoppers. No enemy soldiers. Instead, we're in the middle of a small town at night. Overhead, a row of streetlights illuminates the lawns of suburban homes. Way off in the distance, I see a traffic light flick from red to green. But there are no cars driving down the street. In fact, no movement anywhere. The houses are dark. It's like whoever built this mod forgot to include any people. It's just the two of us. Two heavily armed cyborg soldiers. Standing in the middle of a suburban road. Feeling confused as hell.

I start walking toward an intersection. The detail in this mod is amazing. When I get close enough I can see the letters on the street signs. These ones read *Wentworth Rd.* and *Ancaster Ave.* I have a weird flash of déjà vu. It takes me a second, but then I know where I've seen them before.

[JOSH: follow me] I start jogging down Ancaster. More of the same—quiet streets, sleeping houses. We pass a convenience store closed up for the night. It's neon sign glows above the empty sidewalk.

Then I slide to a stop. We're standing outside a little house, a single-story bungalow. Pretty familiar. In fact, very familiar.

[JOSH: check it out] I watch Griggs's warfighter lumber around the edges of the fence, then turn back to me. [JOSH: look closer]

[GRIGGS: I don't get it. what?] He can't make his warfighter shrug, but I can sense his confusion. I move toward the house, open the gate and walk up to the front door. I stand right under the house number and point my weapon at it.

Then Griggs gets it.

[GRIGGS: 9054 Ancaster? that's your address. this is YOUR house!!! WTF!!!!]

I laugh out loud at the weirdness of it all. Someone put my house into the game—like, the house I'm sitting in. Right now. In real life.

How awesome is that?

[JOSH: it's all here. I think this mod IS Valleytown]

Chapter Four

"King of the world!" shouts Griggs, so loud that his voice gets fuzzed by my headset. His warfighter is standing on top of the church steeple near the center of Valleytown. I'm way down below in the city square. I can see his little arms raised in victory, high above me.

"Using a jetpack to get up there is cheating," I say.

"Cheating? We agreed that the race was to the highest point in Valleytown. We didn't say how to get there."

"Whatever. I didn't know you had a jetpack."

"I upgraded after we won that last campaign. Didn't you?"

The buildings around the center square distract me from his chatter. I've started to notice a few things about the virtual version of Valleytown. Whoever created it has spent a crazy amount of time getting the details right on certain things—like street layouts, and particular neighborhoods. But other parts are undefined. The church, for example, looks like a cardboard cutout shaded in basic gray. The real version has white paint with red trim, ornate stained-glass windows—but there's none of that here. The church clearly wasn't important to whoever made the mod.

"Hello? Earth to Josh?" says Griggs. "I said, look over there."

He's still perched up on the steeple, arm held out like a wind vane. I follow where he's pointing and can just make out a weird blue glow behind a low apartment block to the west.

"I can't see from down here," I say.

"So just fly up here—oh, wait. You can't. Just buy the jetpack next time, will you? I'm coming down." Griggs leaps, rebounds off the church roof and lands on the street below. There's a little flash indicating he's lost some health points from the fall. But we played all last night and for about an hour after school today and still haven't seen anyone else in the mod. We seem to be the only ones here. So I'm not worried about taking damage from doing stupid things like jumping off tall buildings. Nobody is going to try to kill us.

"Follow me," says Griggs. "I saw something cool over there." Our two warfighters stomp down Main Street, past simplified versions of the real stores—Jansen's Hardware, the FrosT-Queen, the bank. It still gives me a weird, dislocated feeling to see real places in here, like I'm in two places at once.

We turn off Main Street onto one that's lined with houses, called Bendis Crescent. Unlike in real life, the houses here are perfectly identical—a single 3-D model that's been "cloned" again and again, creating a row of homes. Each one is labeled with a street number but is otherwise indistinguishable from the others.

Halfway down the street we find one house that is definitely different—it's on fire. Strange blue flames leap out of the windows, flowing around the roofline. The sound of a crackling fire rises in volume as we stop and stare.

"Wow," says Griggs. "I wonder how you do that."

"What do you mean?"

"Well, how do you set stuff on fire? I mean, have you tried blowing anything up in the game yet?"

"Honestly, it hadn't even occurred to me—there are no bad guys here."

"Watch," says Griggs. He turns around and faces a regular home across the street from the burning building. He raises one arm, and a mini-missile the size of a football unpacks from his wrist armor. He squeezes his fist, and the mini-missile leaps forward. It flashes toward the building and detonates in a cloud of smoke and flame. When it clears, the house is still standing. Untouched, as if nothing happened.

"Indestructible. Just like everything in this town. When I was waiting for you to come online tonight, I experimented. Doesn't matter what weapon or what target. Radium gun versus trees. Chain cannon versus windows. Seems like nothing in the game can be destroyed, no matter what you use."

"What about the mod editor?" That's the construction kit that lets you edit objects within the game—kind of like a drawing program in three dimensions.

"Password protected. Can't even open it up. I guess the guy who made the mod is the only one who can change anything."

"So why did he set this place on fire?" We both turn and watch the house continue to burn in the blue inferno. Mind you, the house isn't collapsing or anything. It's like a film loop, a moment of disaster caught on endless replay. Behind a sheet of weird flames, I can make out the house number—*304 Bendis Crescent*. What was so special about this place?

"Follow me!" Griggs suddenly says. "There's something else you need to see!" I watch his warfighter leap down the street, jetpacks flaring. I follow him on the ground, cutting over fences and across lawns to keep up with him. It's settled. Next opportunity, I'm getting a jetpack.

A few minutes later we arrive at the edge of a big complex of buildings. It's been created in the same way the church was. Flat gray angles, like a paper cutout version of a real structure. It's easy enough to figure out what the buildings are, even without the sign out front. McCallum High School.

"Griggs," I say. "You want to spend more time at school? There's got to be something better for us to do."

"Yeah yeah. Follow me inside." His warfighter stomps forward across the flat gray "lawn" to the front doors of the school. I lag behind, looking at a graffiti tag scrawled on an otherwise blank wall—**SUDO**, in black balloon letters. It's weirdly familiar.

"Keep up, will you?" Griggs says. He pushes open the doors, and we walk into the school. We're in the main atrium, hallways branching off to our left and right. It's shadowy in here, so it takes a moment for me to realize that there are a bunch of human figures standing silently in front of us. A crowd of statues.

"I didn't think there were any people in this mod—wait, why aren't they moving?" I say. Griggs's warfighter clicks on his helmet light, and I make mine do the same. We weave the spotlights from figure to figure. The body of each person is either a generic male or female civilian figure, straight out of the basic game. The men are all wearing T-shirts and jeans, and the women are in skirts and tops. But each face is unique. Though distorted and blurred, each one is definitely taken from a real photograph.

"You recognize anyone?" says Griggs. "I think this is the biology teacher."

It takes me a second to realize what's going on.

"Whoever made this place created these people too. He must have taken pictures from Facebook or Instagram or something and pasted them onto the basic characters in the game."

Griggs grunts thoughtfully. "So he built the school, then filled it with his friends?"

"I'm not sure about that." The distorted figures look creepy, anguished. "If he had a bunch of friends, wouldn't they be playing the game with him? Instead, he's got these freaky zombie-doll versions."

Griggs grunts. "Good point."

"Let's get out of here. This is getting strange." I turn around and go back out the main doors.

Over the next few nights Griggs and I explore more of the Valleytown mod. We discover a few cool things. More figures with pasted-on faces taken from photographs—some adults, some kids, nobody that I recognize. Lots of areas that seem to be under construction or abandoned. Roads that simply stop, or half-finished buildings in basic gray cutout form.

Eventually Griggs and I run out of places to explore, so we decide to goof around and climb an electrical tower to get a better view. Just like in real life, these towers are four or five stories tall and made out of cross-hatched metal girders. We race up the tower, then stop at the top, next to the thick power lines that swing out across the void to the next tower. And the next, and the next—a long row of towers stretching across the town. Way off in the distance I see a familiar blue glow again.

"Check it out. There's something else on fire over there." Griggs follows the direction I'm pointing in.

"Yeah, I see it. Let's go." There's a flare of jets from his pack, and he soars away. "Catch me if you can."

Damn. It takes me a while on foot, following the towers until I reach the place where the electrical towers stop and all the power lines converge. This place is really detailed. The mod-maker spent time getting everything just right. There's even a metal fence with a mounted sign near the one gate—*Electrical Substation #32. No Trespassing. Hazard.* A silhouette of a figure being zapped by a lightning bolt. And I understand why they'd want to keep people out. Beyond the fence is a wild nest of electrical cables hung between spidery metal frames. Scattered throughout are towers of black discs and round metal drums. The whole thing crackles occasionally as blue lightning bolts flash from tower to tower.

"Want to go inside?" asks Griggs.

"Are you crazy? That's like a mad scientist's deathtrap in there. Anyway, why would you want to?"

"That is the big question," he says. "Why would you want to build any of this? Who *is* this guy?"

Chapter Five

My routine is the same every day for the
next week. I slide through the school
day like a fish underwater, trying not
to raise a ripple on the surface. Keep
to myself. Face buried in my phone
when I'm not in class, an invisible
shield between me and everybody else.
I see Griggs occasionally as he moves
between his different social groups,

but we connect less and less during school hours. I think he actually enjoys being around everybody in school. For me, it's just a clock ticking down until I can get back to my laptop.

I ride the bus home. I get my homework done as quickly as I can. If Dad's around, there's some small talk. But he wouldn't understand that the best part of my day starts after he goes to bed. That's when I fire up the laptop and visit the virtual Valleytown. Griggs usually shows up for a couple of hours, and we explore. Eventually we come to realize that this mod is a ghost town. There's never been any sign of other players. Never any sign that whoever made this place has returned to it.

Which is fine by me, because it means I can use the place as my private playground. Tonight we're playing an epic game of Capture the Flag through the town. My home base is at the

FrosT-Queen. I'm holed up behind the drive-through window, pinned down by bone-shaking blasts from Griggs's radium gun.

"Give it up!" he yells. Green lightning flashes over my head.

"Come and get it!" I yell back. I know that the walls of the FrosT-Queen are indestructible, just like everything else in the mod. I'm safe as long as I stay below the level of the counter. Then something comes flying through the window and rattles to a stop at my feet. It's a cartoon bomb, a black round ball with a white fuse sticking out the top of it and the word *Boom!* written on the side.

"Seriously?" I say, just as the bomb detonates. My screen flashes red, and I see a picture of my warfighter splattering into a million pixelated bits.

"You like my secret weapon?" Griggs asks. I tap on my keyboard and respawn my character next to his, standing outside the fast-food restaurant.

"Very classy. You make it yourself?" I say.

"Yeah, I used the mod editor."

"You make anything else in here?"

"Not yet. Want to try?" I grunt yes and call up the mod editor. Half my screen still has the in-game view of my war-fighter and the FrosT-Queen. The other half of the screen is filled with green and white letters and numbers. There are options for changing variables within the game, like how hard gravity will pull you down or the position of the sun in the sky. There are also tools for altering the landscape—one that will raise or lower the level of the ground, another that will let you paint surfaces with different textures or colors. I tentatively try a few options on the FrosT-Queen sign. Each click of my mouse is rewarded with the same message.

[Permission denied. Access privileges insufficient.]

I hear Griggs mutter through my headset. "I'm locked out."

"But you made that bomb," I say.

"Yeah. But it was my own possession, right? It's like we can change our own stuff, but not anything in the world around us."

We spend the next hour trying to see if there are any exceptions to this rule.

Which, it turns out, there aren't.

"This sucks, man," says Griggs. "This mod is pretty much abandoned. It's not like anyone cares about it but us. We should be able to tweak it the way we want."

"I agree. It's like salvage rights. You find an abandoned boat, you get to keep it. Same thing. Law of the sea."

"Law of the sea, huh? You spend way too much time learning useless crap, you know that?" says Griggs. "But I agree.

This place is ours now." He pauses, and I watch his warfighter lob a couple of experimental grenade rounds toward the neon *FrosT* letters on the sign. As always, when the smoke clears there's no sign of any damage.

"We need someone with some real skills to unlock this thing. Give us top-level privileges. We need a hacker." He looks at me, and suddenly I see where this is going. "What about that girl you knew in Chicago? She was into programming, right?"

"She was. Still is, I guess. And no, I'm not talking to her."

Griggs's warfighter spins toward me.

"Don't be such a chicken. You said she's been texting you. Jane, right? She wants to talk to you. Give her a call and ask for a little favor."

"You're totally wrong. You don't know what you're talking about."

Problem is, Griggs is totally right. Jane is kind of a genius with computers. She had a job with her dad's tech company as a junior system administrator by the time she was fourteen. If anyone can open up this abandoned piece of software like a can of tuna, it is her.

"I'm going offline. I'll see you tomorrow," I say to Griggs.

"Chicken!" I can hear him clucking at me until I tap the key to disconnect from the game.

I slide my headphones off and rub my eyes. Jane. We grew up across the street from each other, started first grade together, always hung out, played video games together as we got older. Then high school and hormones hit, and what had been a good friendship started to edge toward something more. And then I had to move. Another thing that sucked about Valleytown.

I power up my phone and scroll through the contacts. Jane Yu. Screen name—JANEY. Status—online. I tap the Video camera icon, and green letters pop up on the screen. [Video chat initiated.] And then she's there, looking startled.

"Josh?" She hasn't changed since I last saw her. Black hair pulled back into a tight ponytail. Smooth almond skin, made pale in the light from her laptop screen. She's wearing a black T-shirt, no logo, with a plain silver chain looped around her neck.

"I don't—where have you been?" she says.

"Nowhere. Here," I say. "It's been a while." My fingers drum against my thigh nervously.

"Yeah, it's been about three months and a hundred text messages. Did your phone break? Or they don't have cell reception out in the boonies where you are?"

"It's not like that," I say. "Anyway, I just thought…" I can't do this. "Look, I'll call you back later. I've gotta go."

"Josh, come on." I can see the concern in her eyes. As pissed as she is with me, Jane wants to talk.

"I don't know what you want me to say," I mumble.

"Well, you were pretty clear before we left. We would message each other every day, you said." She fiddles with the silver chain with one hand, twisting and untwisting it.

"And I wanted to," I say. The words start slowly, then tumble out faster. "But it's really weird being out here. After the divorce. After the move. There was nothing familiar, nobody to hang out with. It sucks. It really does. And at first I wanted to call you. I wanted to tell you about it. But then…talking to you was just going to be a reminder of how great things were back in Chicago.

It was easier just to block you out. Block everyone out. It felt, I dunno, safer."

Jane stares at me through the screen. "It sounds like a firewall—you know, the software that stands between your computer and the Internet? You put too many holes in the firewall, you expose yourself to all sorts of trouble. But if you block *everything* out—well, the firewall just becomes a problem. It becomes a prison, not a castle."

"Janey, I don't think I explained it right…" I say.

She leans in toward the camera. "Listen, I'm on the other end of the line, right? But you've got to let me in. I can't do it on my own. Call me when you're ready." I can see her reaching toward her keyboard to disconnect the call.

"Wait!" I say. "I called you for another reason too. I found this site, this mod of *Killswitch*. It's not like anything I've ever seen before. A total recreation of the town I'm living in. Like, everything. My house, my school. I don't know how he did it. Must have taken months."

"Taken who months?" she asks. "Who built it?"

Mysteries and puzzles, preferably related to programming, have always been Jane's kryptonite. She can't help asking more questions. I fill her in as best I can about the virtual Valleytown and its weirdness.

"All right," Jane says eventually. "Text me the details. I'll check it out with you. I'll meet you there tomorrow, five o'clock your time."

"Awesome!" I say, wincing at how eager I sound.

"But be on time," Jane says. "I'm fully expecting you to bail on me. I'm not going to wait around for you."

Chapter Six

The next morning doesn't start well. I slowly open my eyes to see bright sunlight slicing through my closed blinds. Usually when my alarm goes off, my room has a gloomy, cave-like quality to it—not helped by the layer of dirty clothes and comic books littering my floor. But right now the sun is clearly high in the sky, which means…crap. I grab my phone from the bedside table to see what time it is. The screen stays dark. Which means the battery is dead. Which means the alarm didn't go off. I scramble into jeans and a hoodie, grab my backpack and thunder down the stairs. Dad's left the radio in the kitchen going—he's old-school with his technology. But the announcer clues me in about the time.

"…is Newsradio 1430, with our nine o'clock local news. In our top story, fire crews responded last night to a fire on Bendis Crescent that destroyed a family home…"

Nine o'clock. Which means I've missed the bus. Dad's already at work. Which means I'm walking to school. Well, running. I do the math as I start jogging. I have first period off, so if I can get to school by nine thirty-five,

I can avoid a late slip and detention. Because detention means I won't be home by five—and Jane will be gone.

By the time I bang through the double doors of McCallum High, I'm wheezing. Despite the cold October air, my face is covered in a thin layer of sweat. First period has just finished, and the halls are filled with the crush of students. I shove my way through the crowd. Rushing, I carelessly wheel around a corner, and my backpack swings out and smacks a girl in the chest. She turns, shocked expression framed by her flat, blond hair.

"What the hell was that for?" she says. I don't answer, turning away from her and stepping toward the open door of the English classroom just down the hall. Got to make it in there.

"Girl asked a question," says a deep voice. Aaron Carnavon steps in front me. The meathead from the bus.

Valleytown Vikings linebacker. "It's Josh, right?"

"I've got to get to English," I explain. I try to squeeze past him, but he shifts a little, enough to block me.

"Show some class. Apologize to Emily." Over his shoulder, I see Mr. Dyson closing the door to my class-room. Crap.

"Sorry, okay? It's not a big deal," I say and lightly shove Aaron in the chest, trying to get by him. A futile move—the guy is built like a tank.

"Don't make this a big deal," he growls. I duck past him and through the half-closed classroom door. A couple of students look up at me briefly, and a kid with shaggy dark hair smirks at my heavy-breathing arrival as I slide into the seat in front of him. Mr. Dyson furrows his brow at me but doesn't interrupt his lecture. Through the door's window, I see Aaron and Emily walking away down the hallway. So I made it. I wipe my hand over my sweaty face. Barely.

At the end of the school day I'm vomited back out onto the parking lot with the rest of the student body. Griggs finds me in the crowds and we walk, as always, past the pod people to the school buses. We don't talk much, beyond making plans for gaming tonight. I stop midsentence when I see Aaron waiting in the parking lot. I swear and turn around, heading right back into the school.

"What are you doing?" says Griggs, running to catch up. "I thought you needed to get home."

"Yo, Josh!" Aaron yells out. Too late. He's seen me. I slowly turn back around as Aaron limps toward us. "We've got something to discuss." Griggs moves into position between us.

"Aaron!" he says with a big smile. "You coming to Molly's party this weekend? It's going off..." Griggs's voice fades as he sees the furious look on Aaron's face. He turns back to give me a quick glance and says, "What the hell did you do, Josh?"

"I tell you what he did. Josh disrespected my girlfriend. He was all, like, *Get out of my way—big man coming through.* Then he started getting pushy with me. Dude needs to learn some manners."

My heart starts pounding nervously, but I try to keep my voice level. "It wasn't like a big deal or anything. I just bumped into her."

"You hear that, Aaron?" says Griggs. "He said he was sorry."

"That's not what I heard," he growls. "He said it was no big deal."

"Whatever," I say. I can see students filing onto our bus. "This is a waste of time, Griggs." Brave talk, but as I step around Aaron, I'm hoping that he's all talk. Or at least can't catch me with his bad knee. Behind me I can hear Griggs talking him down.

"I'll talk to Josh, all right?" he says. "He can be a total jerk sometimes."

By the time I'm on the bus, it's mostly filled up. Griggs drops into a seat in front of me, then turns around.

"Aaron's a pretty good guy, but you keep pushing his buttons and he'll show up with all his football buddies. Just to make a point. Anyway, you owe me for saving your ass. Twice."

The leftover adrenaline from the face-off with Aaron turns into a sudden rush of anger. My words come out sharp edged.

"Griggs, I don't owe you anything. And I heard you taking his side, calling me a jerk."

"Actually, you *can* be a jerk some-times. It's like you don't know how to deal with people."

"They're pod people, remember? Everybody at this school is like an alien. That's what we said, right?"

"That's not what I meant."

"I don't care what they think, all right?" A couple of guys turn around to look at us, and I realize how loud my voice is.

Griggs looks surprised at the ferocity of my words, then confused. "How can you not care?" he asks.

"I'm not like you," I shoot back. "I don't need to be friends with everyone. And I don't need you fighting my battles for me."

"All right. See how that works out for you." He snorts, then turns away to face the front of the bus. "You're on your own, Josh."

Chapter Seven

It's down to the wire, but I make it online by 4:58 PM. My warfighter waits in the main square, near the church. The game has shifted into nighttime mode again. The windows glow warmly in the storefronts, and the streetlights spread puddles of light down the length of Main Street. A flat moon hovers above a slightly pixelated tree line in the distance.

There's the sizzling sound that indicates someone new is joining the game. I spin my warfighter around and see her, a different version of my soldier, dressed in dark-blue armor with a long sniper rifle slung across her back.

"You made it!" I say into my headset.

Jane's voice crackles back to me. "Don't sound so surprised. *I* always show up." Ouch. But her voice softens. "Anyway, let's see what you've got."

We tour around Valleytown as I explain the discoveries Griggs and I have made, like the school filled with cutout figures. We end up at the burning house on Bendis Crescent.

"And all these places actually exist? Like, this house?" she asks, as we watch flames snap and writhe around the building.

"I think so. I mean, I haven't actually gone to this address." As I say it, I have another moment of déjà vu. Something about a fire on Bendis—where did I hear that?

Jane interrupts my train of thought. "And you don't know who made this?"

"No clue. And I've never seen anyone else in here. It's like a ghost town. Nothing moves except for us."

"Weird," Jane says. "Crazy. And kind of awesome. I'm glad you showed me."

"Me too. I almost didn't, you know? I thought you might not be into it."

Her warfighter turns toward me, the flames from the burning house reflecting off the smooth metal surfaces of her armor.

"So what made you change your mind?" she says.

"Griggs, actually. I told him you were a kick-ass coder, and he thought maybe you could help us figure out how to get access privileges to mod things in here. We're locked out."

There's a pause before she answers me. "You're unbelievable."

"What?"

"*That's* why you got in touch with me? After all the times I reached out to you? You wanted to play in your sandbox here and needed me to give you the keys? You care more about this game than you do about me."

"It's not like that—"

"It is exactly like that," she says and swings the sniper rifle off her back. She takes aim and fires two quick shots into my warfighter's head. The view shifts crazily as my character collapses. A red *X* appears above my head. I tap furiously on the keyboard, trying to resurrect myself as quickly as possible.

"Jane?" I call out, but she's broken the audio link. By the time I get my warfighter back on his feet, Jane's character has vanished from the game as well. I wander around the empty streets of Valleytown for a while, looking for her. But I know I've blown it. She's really gone.

An hour later my phone trembles on the desk beside my laptop. It's a text from Jane.

Got into mod server, gave you root-level access. Should be able to change whatever you want in the game now.

Awesome. And maybe she's not that mad? I chew on my lip, thinking. I don't want to blow it again by saying the wrong thing, so I just send back the simplest thing I can think of.

Thx.

She texts me back immediately.

You've got your stupid game. *Blip.* Another one.

But you don't have me. *Blip*.
Goodbye, Josh.

I take a heavy breath. Pick up the phone, scroll to her contact. Look at the glowing green Phone icon. Should I call her, fix this before it becomes something permanent and awful? I watch the clock at the top of phone's screen click through the minutes. I feel like a computer that's locked up, a little icon in my head spinning and spinning. Frozen. For the millionth time, I realize I don't know how to do this...stuff with people. I wish there was code that explained it, that I could rewrite conversations. Rebuild relationships like I can fix buildings in *Killswitch*.

Frustration starts to bubble into anger. I put the phone down on the desk, hard. Then log back into *Killswitch*. My warfighter appears in the Valleytown central square. Still a quiet summer night.

There's a blue van parked right in front of me. A generic type I've seen scattered around the game.

Jane. Griggs. I don't need them. With a grunt, I punch the side of the virtual van. The entire side of the van caves in. I stare at it stupidly. That wasn't supposed to happen.

Up until now, everything in the game was indestructible. Jane has changed the rules for me.

I raise my radium gun at Jansen's Hardware store and squeeze the trigger. A brilliant burst of green lightning slams into the big plate-glass window. The deafening roar rattles through my headset, and the entire store vanishes in a cloud of flames and smoke. Chunks of debris arc out of the explosion. I turn to a tree next to me and switch to flame-thrower. There's a satisfying *whoomp* as the tree ignites. I start walking down Main Street, lobbing grenades at houses, stores, cars—anything in my path. I don't care.

Blowing crap up should make me feel better. Instead I start to feel even angrier. Then I realize why. Nothing is fighting back. I want something to take me on. And then it occurs to me that if Jane gave me admin rights, I can create anything I want. Not just destroy.

I stop at an intersection and put away my weapons. Tapping a few keys, I pull up the mod editor. Just like before, my screen splits in two—half of it has the in-game view of my warfighter, while the other half is filled with options for changing the variables of the game. I click on the toggles to generate a new creature and a message pops up:

[Permission granted. You have root-access privileges.]

A black mechanical spider appears next to my warfighter in the middle of the street. I give it a pair of laser cannons—not too powerful—then switch back to game mode to activate it.

The spider leaps at my warfighter, locking onto my chest with powerful legs. I press my fist into its underbelly and unload my mini-missile into it. The spider detonates satisfyingly, chunks flying onto nearby lawns.

I smile. Destroy. Create. Time to make some changes around here.

Chapter Eight

I sometimes imagine my life as the pages from a comic book.

Panel 1.

Black and white. Me at school, frowning. The teacher—a bug-eyed monster—yammers in the background. There are little thought bubbles floating above my head as I dream up new things to create in *Killswitch*.

Panel 2.

Black and white. Me walking home, frowning, past crowds of students. I've become half invisible, faded out. They all ignore me, even Griggs. But I don't notice. My thought bubbles are starting to fill the panel with spiderbots, bugchoppers, warfighters.

Panel 3.

Black and white. The thought bubbles have grown again, crowding everything else off the page. People run screaming from my monsters.

Panel 4.

Full color. Me, dark bags under my eyes from sleep deprivation. Sitting in front of my laptop. The ideas from my thought bubbles are now contained on the screen. Becoming real. Big smile on my face. The sun is rising as I finish another epic addition to my new world.

The panels repeat, again and again. Eleven days and nights pass by like this.

Each day, my virtual world grows bigger and more beautiful. And the real world just seems to get dimmer.

Chapter Nine

On day twelve, it's Halloween. More important, it's when I get the idea for my fortress. Something with thin steel towers like knives. A blade castle. The pencil sketches on blue-lined paper in my binder don't look like much. But they have potential. I'm not sure where to put it in the game though. Build it over top of my real address? Or maybe put it right in the middle of Havenwood Park—that might fit the castle vibe better. I casually cover the whole thing up with my textbook as Mr. Dyson wanders down my aisle, but he's busy talking about Greek myths. Across the aisle Griggs is flipping his pen between his fingers, a nervous habit I've seen him do before. He scribbles something down on a scrap of paper. When Dyson isn't looking, he throws the folded-up note over to me.

Don't be a wangster. LAN party with the guys after school. I'll get pizza.

I crumple up the note, shaking my head. Why doesn't he get it? I don't want to hang out with anybody else. I don't need anybody else.

Later, dinner with Dad. Over-reheated spaghetti, he asks me the mandatory questions. How my day was, if I have any homework—stuff I know he feels he has to ask me in order to be a good parent. And I give him the basic answers.

Ones that won't raise any alarms. Definitely not telling him how I'm gradually unplugging from everybody. Plugging into the game.

"You're not going trick-or-treating tonight, are you?" he grunts. I shake my head, keeping my eye on the noodles twisted in the red sauce on my plate. Like tentacles. Hey, there's an idea. I can add tentacles to the tank I'm designing.

"Good. You're too old for that kid stuff. Like those video games. Kid stuff."

I shake my head again. Keep quiet and get out as soon as I can.

Later I'm on my second can of Monster Juice, and the caffeine is hissing through my veins. The beat of my tunes wraps around me like a heartbeat. On the laptop screen images are flashing by at high speed as I type sequences of commands into a text window. Plates of metal melt together to form the sharp-edged walls of my castle. I clone my robot spider design until an army of them waits for me in the dungeon below. Spiked tentacles slide into the armored skin of a command tank, creating a nightmare combination of squid and machine. It reminds me of the sea monster from Norse mythology that Mr. Dyson was talking about in class—a Kraken. A Kraken tank. Awesome.

And then everything freezes.

I swear quietly, hoping I haven't lost the last set of changes I made to my designs. I reboot the laptop and see what happens. Everything seems fine until I try to reconnect to the Valleytown mod, and that's when a message appears.

[Permission denied.]

I stare at the words dumbly for a moment. Did I do something in the editor that messed things up? I carefully repeat my steps, making sure that I do everything correctly. But the response on the screen is the same.

[Permission denied.]

Crap. I can suddenly feel my pulse in my forehead. So many hours of work on all these special creations. Buildings. Creatures. Weapons. Everything I created in the Valleytown mod—lost?

My phone suddenly vibrates against the desk. A text message.

u don't belong.

From someone named Sudo. Sudo? Why does that name seem familiar? Oh yeah, the graffiti at school. And in the game.

Who is this?? I text back. A minute goes by with no response. I'm just starting to put the phone down when it vibrates again.

i own Valleytown & u don't belong & stay out

You created the mod?

i made it and u messed it up, Sudo texts.

Wait—what? Before I can type a response, another message arrives.

how did u do it? i did not give u permission

None of this is making sense. How did this person get my cell number? It's not Jane—she's too pissed at me to mess around like this, and it's not her style. The only other person who would try something like this would be—oh, I get it.

This you, Griggs? Not funny

There's a long pause. Then a flurry of messages.

not griggs

how did u mess up my game?

u tell me NOW, josh, or i will make u pay

Okay. This isn't sounding like Griggs. Or Jane. Or anyone else I know. So who the hell is it?

How did you get my number? I type slowly.

i know who u are, he texts.

Sean Rodman

I drop the phone on my desk and back away like it might contaminate me. I walk over to the window of my room and look out. The view is just like it was the last time I was in the game—nighttime with a crescent moon hanging over the city. Except here, in the real world, there are kids in costumes walking from house to house. Laughter. Life. In the mod there aren't any people. Except for me.

And Sudo.

The creepy feeling comes back. I quickly pull the curtains closed.

The phone starts to vibrate rhythmically on my desk. It's a phone call this time, not a text message. I slowly walk back to the desk and turn it over. I don't recognize the number. But I'm certain it's Sudo. My finger hangs over the green Answer icon. Part of me wants to ignore him. Part of me is afraid to.

I stab the green icon and put the phone to my ear.

"Who is this?" I say quietly. The voice on the other end is disguised, warped into robot-like tones. But I can also detect something else. Something unexpected. He sounds worried, nervous.

"You don't get to know," Sudo says. "Tell me how you got admin permission for the mod. I need to fix the security and…just explain where the hole is. I don't want anyone else to get in and mess it up. I just want to keep it…the way it is."

Suddenly I understand what he's feeling. He wants to protect his kingdom, where no one else is allowed.

"I didn't wreck anything," I say. "I just built some new stuff—"

Sudo snorts. "You trashed half the downtown with your little fragfest.

I had to reload all the data from an older copy. Took me two hours to make sure everything was right again."

"Okay, you're right. That's on me." I sit down heavily in my desk chair, phone feeling clammy against my ear. "But I really don't want to destroy anything else. I like the mod. It's cool. I just want to play in it. Build stuff. Like the castle."

"Castle?" From the surprised tone in Sudo's voice, I realize that he hasn't yet found Blade Castle stashed in Havenwood Park. "It's not your playground. Forget it—just stay out." He sounds like he's about to disconnect. Crap!

"I'll make you a deal," I say quickly. "Let me in the game again, and I'll explain how I did it. Show you everything I've done. But only once I'm in the game with you."

The connection crackles a little bit. Finally he answers.

"All right. Log in." The phone beeps, and the call is terminated.

I turn back to my laptop and try connecting to the mod again. The cursor pulses blue and green for a moment. Then, with a shower of pixels, my warfighter appears in the central square of Valleytown.

I'm back in. And this time, I'm not alone.

Chapter Ten

The game is still in night mode, with the moon still hanging in the same position in the sky. In the cold blue light, towering over me at twice my height, stands a mecha-golem. Shaped roughly like a human, the thing is a wild combination of parts. It's cobbled together from the leftover pieces of a hundred different creatures. Its left hand is a cruel-looking hook, which it raises slowly to point down the street.

I turn my warfighter and start walking, the mecha-golem falling into step beside me. As we walk through the downtown, I notice that the destruction I caused last time has been fully erased. As if nothing ever happened.

After a few minutes we arrive at the electrical substation that Griggs first led me to. Lightning still crackles along wires strung between the massive transformers. After a moment a strange figure emerges from the shadows beneath one of the towers. He's wearing warfighter armor bigger and heavier than my own.

"Sudo?" I ask. "Is this your... home?"

"My fortress," he says. His voice isn't masked and distorted like it was on the phone. He sounds human. And prouder, more sure of himself. "So let's see what you built. What are the coordinates? We'll fly there."

"Ah, that's a problem. I don't have a jetpack."

"That's lame," he snorts. "Hang on for a second." I hear the faint clicking of keys through the headset. A few seconds later the image of my warfighter alters as two jet pods appear on his back. Cool.

"Thanks," I say reflexively. We sort out the location coordinates of the castle, then launch our warfighters into the night sky. The mecha-golem and the electrical towers quickly dwindle beneath us. Valleytown is spread out below like a map, roads outlined by the dots of streetlights. Homes glow in the darkness. But nothing moves. In real life, the headlights of cars would crawl down the streets. Little knots of people would be clustered around the shops.

There would be the noise of arguments and accidents, life being lived messily. Not here. Everything is static. Like a beautiful photograph, a snapshot, a perfect version of a screwed-up world.

Sudo interrupts my thoughts. "You going to talk now?" he asks impatiently. "Tell me how you made yourself an admin?"

"Honestly, I didn't," I say, tensing up a little. Not sure how he's going handle this next part. "I had a friend do it for me."

Sudo's warfighter suddenly spins in midair to face me. "What? Someone else was in my mod?"

"Two people," I say, hoping my staying calm will encourage Sudo not to freak out. "A friend of mine from school was playing in here with me for a while. And then someone else hacked your system and gave me admin rights. I don't really know how she did it."

There's silence from Sudo, his war-fighter hovering in the dark sky. I realize how pissed he must be. I would be if I were him.

"Neither one is coming back," I say quietly.

"How can you be sure?" he says.

"We're not friends anymore. They're gone for good."

There's a pause. Then Sudo's war-fighter turns and hits some kind of turbo-boost, rapidly disappearing into the distance. I engage my jets and race after him.

I finally catch up with him at the park. I land beside his warfighter, standing on the ground looking up at the sharp-edged spires of my black metal castle. A swarm of spiderbot scouts, the size and shape of hockey pucks, come skittering over the walls to examine us. I've programmed them to recognize me and not attack—but I can tell they're not sure about Sudo.

"Uh, better take a step back," I warn him. "Those little guys aren't bad on their own. But they'll call out the big guns eventually." Sudo's warfighter shuffles back. He turns slowly, taking it all in.

"You did all this?" He doesn't sound angry anymore, just kind of mystified.

"Took me about two weeks. There's lots more inside."

"It's…cool," Sudo says reluctantly. "So show me the rest."

I disable the spiderbot defenses, then bring down the obsidian drawbridge. We walk into the castle and toward the great hall. This is where I've assembled the big mechanical spiders and Kraken tanks, lined up neatly in rows. We look over them from an upper balcony. Occasionally a little dragonfly-bot clicks through the air, carrying pieces of equipment to the multi-armed mechanic. In turn, the mechanic assembles the pieces into more bots. A little factory creating my pet monsters. Sudo's warfighter watches the mechanic for a long time. When he finally speaks, he doesn't sound mad, just kind of perplexed.

"Everything in this game was made by me, do you understand? It was all part of my plan. I never wanted anyone else to build in it. None of this belongs here." Sudo's warfighter lifts his gun, pointing at the mechanic. At the spiderbots. Then at me. "You don't belong here."

I make my warfighter back up a few steps. "Look, I can't stop you from destroying any of this. Or kicking me out. Like I said, the one other person who could give me admin rights to the game is gone. And she's not coming back. You lock me out, and I'm gone forever."

Sudo says nothing. But orange lines on the barrel of his gun start to pulse, indicating that the weapon is armed. I quickly continue with my speech.

"But you've made something amazing here. Something that's like the real world—but better. And I think I can add to it. Maybe it wasn't part of what you had planned. But you like what I've built, right?"

Sudo grunts. "Yeah."

"So why not give me a chance to show you that I belong here?"

The gun doesn't waver. The orange lights pulse faster.

"I belong here, Sudo," I say.

There's a pause that feels like forever. Finally the orange glow fades from his weapon.

"Maybe," Sudo says. "But you have to prove yourself first."

Chapter Eleven

Sudo's warfighter leads me back outside. We move past the bustling bugchoppers and spiderbots, down the rows between the hulking Kraken tanks.

"Why do you think I built Valleytown?" he asks.

"I don't know," I say. "A place to hang out? Kind of like a better version of the real world?"

"No," Sudo snorts. "That would be stupid. I built Valleytown so I could have a place to test things out."

"Things?"

"Ideas. Plans. Missions." His warfighter spins to face me. "You're going on a mission. It's going to be a little different than what you're used to. If you can handle it, I'll let you stick around." I hear the muffled clicking sound of Sudo typing commands on his keyboard.

"What do—" I start to ask. But before I can finish, everything changes. The castle vanishes, and suddenly I'm back in the central Valleytown square, next to the church. Same moon. Same downtown.

I see something move in the distance. A figure. Then another. Dark silhouettes shuffle toward me. A faint groaning fills the air. Zombies? Must be zombies.

I know how to handle this—I've been trained by a hundred video games,

TV shows and movies. See, your basic zombie is dumb and slow. Not a problem for a warfighter when it's one-on-one. The only problem is that zombies rarely come alone. Instead you get swarms that need to be mowed down like blades of grass. I warm up my radium gun and get to work. Green lightning crackles from the barrel, snapping into the crowd of shadowy figures. I hit one, and he glows green, then brightens to an unbearable white. Then vanishes. My score increases a few points. I move the crosshairs on the screen to my next shadowy target. Zap.

But more and more keep coming at me. Main Street is filling up with the groaning horde. I keep firing, but my radium gun eventually runs out of charges. When I pause to reload, things go to hell. Like water surging over a broken dam, the wave of zombies rushes inexorably toward my warfighter. Time to go.

I spin around and run smack into Mr. Dyson.

I gasp. What's standing in front of me isn't a classic video-game zombie. Instead, it's like the zombie dolls that Griggs and I found in the virtual version of our high school. A basic black-and-gray human-shaped figure with an actual photograph pasted onto the head. In this case, Mr. Dyson's. His image must have been taken from the school website. The effect might be funny if it weren't so creepy. His face is stretched in a weird permanent grin, unmoving and malevolent. His arms reach out and claw at my warfighter. The screen flashes red as I start to lose health points.

"Sorry, Mr. Dyson," I mutter. I squeeze off a burst from the radium gun, and he vanishes in a green haze. The groaning suddenly sounds louder, and I turn around. Dozens of figures lurch toward me, almost within arm's reach.

Now that they are closer, I can see that each zombie is actually created in the same way as Mr. Dyson was—a basic human shape with a photograph pasted over the head. Some of the faces I recognize from school—students, teachers. All real people.

Sudo is putting real people in the game. And getting me to blow them away.

I raise my radium gun. Then my finger hesitates over the trigger button on my game controller. The zombie dolls shamble closer.

"You know what you have to do, right?" Sudo's voice makes me jump. His warfighter is nowhere to be seen, but he must be watching me somehow. He sounds peeved. "Just kill them all. The next part of the mission is even better."

I just stare at the weird crowd as it shuffles toward my warfighter, scanning

the faces. The goth kid from the bus.
A couple of teachers.

Griggs.

Both my hands drop away from the
keyboard. The screen starts strobing red
as the zombie dolls surround my warfighter, clawing at his armor. But I do
nothing. Within a few seconds the red X
is hovering in the air, and my warfighter
is dead.

"What the hell happened?" Sudo says.
"You should have slaughtered them!"

I answer slowly, processing it all.
"Yeah, zombies are usually easy to
slaughter. But these ones were different."

"The faces? That's what makes it
awesome."

"But they were like real people," I
say slowly.

"Was that the problem?" Sudo
sounds genuinely puzzled.

"I don't know."

There's a long pause. "Maybe I was right. You don't get it. You don't belong here." I hear a muffled tapping sound as Sudo starts keying in commands. My screen switches from the mod to the main screen.

"Wait!" I say. "It wasn't the faces. That part was really cool." I try to say it with an enthusiasm I don't feel.

"So what happened?"

"It was just my Internet connection. It gets laggy sometimes, makes things freeze up. Just a glitch."

There's another pause. I'm not sure he believes me. I still feel weirdly queasy about what I saw. Like I just picked at a bandage and saw a little bit of the infection waiting underneath. Part of me is hoping he just kicks me out.

But he doesn't.

"I get it," he says. "Lag sucks. Try rebooting and logging in. We'll do it again."

I rub my forehead. "Tomorrow, okay? Can we do it then? The connection might be better."

"Yeah, sure," Sudo says, yawning. "It's late anyway. See you tomorrow night."

"Great," I say, relieved.

"Or maybe I'll see you at school." Sudo's laugh is like rough sandpaper on stcel. "But I bet you won't see me."

Chapter Twelve

Sunlight punctures the cracks around my window blinds, sending laser-like lines onto my bed. Right into my eyes. I can't help but wake up, despite only having had three hours' sleep. But it's the smell of bacon from the kitchen downstairs that actually gets me out of bed.

"Morning," grunts Dad. He's wearing pyjama bottoms and an old Rangers T-shirt, standing at the stove. A pan of bacon sizzles beside another of bright-yellow scrambled eggs. "I'm coming off the night shift. Thought we could both use breakfast before you head off to school."

I point at a glass of OJ on the table. "This for me?"

"Yup. Grab some forks?" My dad is a lousy cook—except for breakfast. He's got it down to an art, and within minutes we're both enjoying grease, protein and coffee. The perfect way to start the day.

Pushing his now-empty plate away, Dad looks at me over his mug. "You got something to want to say to me?"

All that good food suddenly flops over in my stomach. "What do you mean?" I say carefully.

"I've been working a lot recently." He takes a sip of his coffee. "Nights. Weekends. Probably too much. Tricky arson cases—like that one on Bendis that was on the news? Anyway, I'm the new guy, so everyone else piles the paperwork on me. I'm pretty sure you think I'm not paying attention to you anymore." His eyes narrow.

"That's a bad thing?" I risk a joke.

But Dad laughs, more of a gravelly bark. "Listen, that fight we had the other night, some of the things you said—I know the move hasn't been easy. The stuff with your mom wasn't easy. And I haven't made it any easier for you since then. So I guess what I'm saying is, you've got a right to be pissed with me. With everything."

I just nod.

"But here's the thing." His gray eyes bore into mine. "I want you to trust that everything I've done is because I want the best for you. Trust that I'm on your side, always."

When did Dad get so touchy-feely? But I can see from his eyes that he means it. He's actually worried about me or something. Anyway, it's making me feel weird. Nervous.

"I've got to get to the bus." I get up and put my dishes in the sink. "I'll see you tonight?"

He sighs and shakes his big, bear-like head. "Best I can do is frozen dinner for you. I'm out on the second shift. Three PM to eleven PM. But how about we do breakfast again tomorrow?"

The sleep deprivation is hitting me hard, so I rest my head against the cool, smooth metal of my locker. The bell rings, startling me upright as students flood into the central hallway. I stand still while they rush around me, trying to study each face as it floats past. It feels like I'm in slow motion and everything else is in fast-forward. Man, my head is in a strange space. But I keep studying faces. Trying to figure out which one is Sudo.

You know what's the worst time of day when you haven't had enough sleep? Right after lunch. Of course, it's Mr. Dyson's class. He's lecturing about some Greek legend, Narcissus and Nemesis. Cool names. But no matter what I do, my eyelids keep slamming down like metal shutters over my eyes. And then I have these vivid flashes of the zombie dolls from last night. I can't look Mr. Dyson in the eye, which is stupid. It was just a game.

Only something about it doesn't feel like just a game.

Finally, desperate to stay awake, I stick up my hand and ask to go to the bathroom. I splash cold water on my face, then stare at my image in the mirror. Heavy dark bags under my bloodshot eyes. I look like crap, I think. Then I see Griggs looking over my shoulder in the mirror, apparently reading my mind.

"You do look like crap," he says. "Just in case, y'know, you weren't a hundred percent certain."

"Thanks a bunch." I don't turn around as he comes over to the sinks to wash his hands.

"Don't mention it. I figure you've decided to take some seriously hard drugs. Bad idea, by the way. Or maybe you donated blood—like, a couple gallons of it? Also a bad idea." He raises an eyebrow. "Or you've been playing *Killswitch* around the clock?"

I can't help but laugh a little. "That would be my addiction of choice."

"Always was. You still playing in the Valleytown mod?"

"Yeah," I say. "I built some amazing things in there. Totally owned it." I thump the dispenser to get some towels and start patting my face dry. "Anyway, I'm thinking about stopping."

"Really? Why?"

I look at Griggs. Messy brown hair frames his chubby face, his eyes curious behind thick black-framed glasses. Then, for a second, I see his face on the zombie thing again.

"I can't explain." I walk quickly out of the bathroom.

The day finally ends. A headache has spent the last hour or so sprouting behind my forehead. I hustle across the parking lot, eyes down, earbuds on.

Blocking everything out. That's why I don't hear the car coming at me, just see a last-second flash of metal and glass out of the corner of my eye. Then I'm looking down at a car bumper just an inch away from my jeans. I raise my eyes to look through the windshield. It's Aaron Carnavon. He leans out the driver's-side window.

"You stepped right out in front of me! What the hell are you doing?"

A crowd of students has suddenly materialized—a cross-section of the pod people are watching us. They're all here to watch a fight, I realize. To watch me get pounded into the ground. But Aaron doesn't even get out of the car. He just shakes his head, looking confused and a little disgusted.

"Just stay out of my way, freak. I know who you are. But I don't know what your problem is." He reverses the car, then accelerates around and past me.

A muscle in my thigh keeps twitching uncontrollably, nervous shock from the near miss. I walk home carefully, not quite trusting myself.

Chapter Thirteen

I take my half-warmed-up dinner in a plastic tray to my bedroom and sit down in front my laptop. I stare at the blank screen for a few minutes, chewing on beef stroganoff and peas. What I said to Griggs was true—I am thinking about finding a new game. I don't have to play in Sudo's world.

Except it was my world too. Part of me liked the power. Liked the idea of creating a reality where I could control everything. In a way the real world will never allow.

I punch the Power button on the laptop. It hums to life. By the time I log into the Valleytown mod, Sudo is already waiting for me.

"Where have you been?" He sounds peeved.

"Sorry." Jeez, it was only a few minutes past our agreed time. "Are we going to do that zombie killing mission again?"

"Not exactly." I hear the sound of keys tapping in my headset, and suddenly my warfighter is inside a building. It takes a second for me to recognize the gray-black cardboard structure. The long hall with doorways puncturing it at regular intervals.

"This is McCallum High?"

"Uh-huh." There's a beep, and all the doors open. Zombie dolls stumble out into the hallway from the adjoining rooms. I start tapping commands into my keyboard to arm my weapons system.

"Stand down. Easy, man," says Sudo. "Your mission is just to follow one guy. I'll give you more instructions on the way." A single figure is outlined in white, making it easy to track him through the crowds. I nudge the controls, and my warfighter starts to trail him.

We go up and down the stairs, into rooms and back out again. It feels like the figure is moving randomly but is always just far enough away that I have to stay on my toes to keep up. I try to make out the face plastered onto the doll's head, but I never quite get a good angle.

"Are you just yanking my chain?" I say. "Is there a point to this?"

Sudo just laughs.

Finally my target wanders out of the school and into the parking lot outside. A row of identical cars lines one side of the lot. To my surprise, the zombie doll gets into one of them. The car backs out, then starts to drive away.

"Don't lose him!" says Sudo. "You'll mess this up."

"Okay, okay." I trigger my jetpack and soar up above the trees. It takes a second to regain my view of the car. I'm hovering right overhead as it cruises down Levy Street. After a few minutes it pulls into a driveway. The zombie gets out and walks into the nearby house.

"Okay, new mission objective. Land, and destroy the vehicle. Defend yourself against any counter-response," says Sudo. I can hear the excitement in the clipped way he's speaking, like he's mission control on a space flight or something. I cut the jets and drop to the driveway beside the car. I take a good look at it. It's one of the regular cars used in all the *Killswitch* games. Nothing fancy.

"This doesn't make any sense. Why am I doing this?"

"Just do it. Play the game. Complete the mission."

I shake my head. Whatever. It's less creepy than taking out the zombies. The question is, radium cannon or mini-missile? I pull up my weapon inventory. Instead of my regular arsenal, there's only one option.

"Pipe bomb?" I say out loud. I've never seen that one before. Must be something Sudo made, like the cartoon bomb Griggs created ages ago.

"Come on, come on," Sudo says.

I select the bomb and see that my warfighter is now clutching a little stick in his hand. It takes a second for me to figure out how to arm it. Then I plant it under the car. A moment later there's a flash, and a cloud of smoke roils up from the car. When it disappears, the car is engulfed in blue flames.

"Awesome!" I say. "Now what?" But before Sudo can answer, the front door of the house bursts open and the zombie driver comes charging back out. I pull up my weapon inventory, but there's nothing left in it. Crap. The zombie is on top of me a second later, my screen strobing red as health points drop with each clawing attack. I struggle to maneuver my warfighter out from under the zombie. I finally catch a glimpse of the thing's face. A photograph of Aaron Carnavon.

Suddenly I feel rage and frustration come boiling out of me, like a dam breaking. In that moment, I just want to destroy Aaron. Destroy all the pod people. Clean them all out of Valleytown, leaving it perfect and empty. I shove Aaron back toward the burning car.

Into the inferno. Blue flames leap out and consume him. I realize I'm shouting a weird war cry, and Sudo joins in.

"That was awesome!" shouts Sudo through my headset. "That was for you, man! Didn't that feel good?"

Too good. My voice is hoarse from shouting. "How do you know about him and me?"

I can practically hear Sudo rolling his eyes. "I've been watching you. I saw everything in the parking lot today. Okay, next mission. I'll start you back at McCallum and—"

"No, wait. I have to—" My hands are trembling on the controller. I put it gently down on my desk.

"We'll play tomorrow." Sudo's voice is firm.

"I don't know—"

"You're not getting it, Josh. We *will* play tomorrow. And you're missing the best part. This was just a training mission." His voice drops. "Tomorrow is for real."

"What do you mean?"

"I told you." He sounds like a teacher, annoyed that his student isn't paying attention. "I created the Valleytown to test out plans. To train for missions. Practice runs. Check it out."

My warfighter dissolves in a spray of pixels, then reappears in front of the house perpetually engulfed in blue flames. The sign in front reads *304 Bendis Crescent.*

"This is Mrs. Cormer's house. The biology teacher? It took me weeks of practice in the game to get the details right on this one. How to ignite the fire so it would spread quickly. Which direction to approach from the street so that nobody could see me."

"Wait, that was you? You actually did it?" I say weakly. "In real life? Why?"

"Because she failed me out of biology."

"That's…" My words trail off.

Sudo laughs. "Don't freak out. I'm not that crazy. I planned it so that nobody was home at the time. But I taught her a lesson, didn't I? And tomorrow we'll teach Aaron a lesson too. We'll torch that car of his."

I sit silently, watching the house burn on the screen.

"You still in?" Sudo asks.

You're actually insane, I want to say. *And I'm insane for not pulling the plug right now.*

I want to blame it on being freaked out. On surprise. On shock.

But maybe part of me actually wants to help him. Control the world, just like we control the game.

Either way, Sudo takes my hesitation for agreement.

"I'll text you the details about where to pick up the—"

His voice cuts out as I slap the laptop shut. What have I done?

Chapter Fourteen

The vertical blinds divide the cold autumn sunlight into bars on my ceiling. My eyes feel crusty and tired. I was thinking about Sudo and the Valleytown mod all night. The righteous anger I felt when I pushed the Aaron zombie into his own flaming car. How easy it was to let anger be the only emotion I felt toward Aaron. Toward everybody.

Like anger was my firewall, my shield. Only it doesn't feel right. Sudo has gone down that road. Jane said a firewall could become a prison to contain you rather than a castle to protect you.

My phone buzzes. I know who it is before I swipe the screen awake.

i will give u the item for your inventory for the mission. meet me noon in cafeteria, last table on right. be alone.

I feel a sick lurch in my stomach as I think about the "item" he's talking about. The one weapon in my inventory from the game last night. The pipe bomb? A real one?

understood?

I stare at the little screen like it's a snake about to bite me. I can't hide from Sudo. I can't just run away. He won't let me. But I don't want to play anymore. I don't want anyone to actually get hurt because of his sick games. I hear the rattle of pots downstairs as Dad makes breakfast. And I have an idea. Finally I tap a single letter.

K

When I emerge in the kitchen downstairs, the scene looks weirdly normal in comparison to what's going on in my head. Dad has the bacon on the table, and the warm tang of coffee is in the air. The newspaper rustles as he lowers it to watch me fix a cup of coffee.

"Morning." He studies me. "You all right?"

I just shake my head no and drop into the seat across from him. We lock eyes, and I know I've triggered his cop instincts. He doesn't raise his voice. Just folds the newspaper neatly and rests it on the table.

"What's going on?" he says gently. Like he doesn't want to scare me off.

Like maybe he knows things are really bad this time.

"You said you want me to trust you, right?" I say. "Well, I need you to trust me. And do something for me."

"Joshua, what's going on?" He says the words carefully.

"I can't tell you yet. You have to trust me." Dad's face is completely still, his eyes fixed on mine. Finally, he nods.

"What do you need?"

"Meet me at the school parking lot today. At noon."

I look at the digital numbers of the clock mounted to the cafeteria wall: *11:58*. I can hear the thud of my heartbeat inside my head, but I'm trying to look calm. Still, I jump when Griggs drops his cafeteria tray onto the table with a rattle of cutlery.

"You still look like crap," he says, sitting down across from me. "But I've decided that I'm not going to let you sit alone anymore. You are literally going to have to pick me up and move me." He looks at me defiantly.

"You can't be here," I say.

"I know," says Griggs, holding up his hands in protest. "You don't need any stinking friends. You're the original lone wolf." I shoot him a dark look, but he only continues on. "You can be a jerk all you want, but I'm still worried about you. I'm pretty sure I am your only friend in here, and like I said before, it's a combat zone. You need someone to watch your back. I'm your bodyguard. Except I think I'm protecting you from yourself."

"No, seriously. Get the hell out of here," I hiss. I look around at the crowd. Nobody is walking toward me. No sign of Sudo.

"I can't hear you," Griggs says, miming plugging his ears.

The clock on the wall flashes *12:00*.

"Griggs, I mean it. Go!" He just leans back in his chair, confused.

"Chill out, Josh. Seriously, take a pill."

My phone vibrates in my pocket. I pull up the message and feel cold prickling up and down the back of my neck.

not what we planned

I look around the cafeteria, scanning the crowd of students hunched over their lunches, standing in the aisles. Which one is he?

Not my fault. one more chance. meet in parking lot?

I grab my backpack and stand up while I'm still texting. Leaving a stunned Griggs behind me, I shove my way through the crowd until I slam open the doors to the parking lot. I slowly turn in a circle. Where is he?

"Josh," a voice says, and I turn around. He's my height, shaggy dark hair framing a thin, pale face. Eyes like black beads, focused intently on my face. I've seen him around, but he was always in the background. Just part of the crowd of pod people.

Sudo smiles. "I knew you'd want to play my game."

At that moment Griggs comes up behind Sudo and yells at me. "Dude, now I am seriously pissed! There really is something wrong with—who is this?"

A look of surprise, then fury flashes across Sudo's face. "You were supposed to be alone!"

Sudo shoulders me aside and starts running across the parking lot. I drop my backpack and chase after him. We're halfway across the lot when I hear a car door slam and a voice barks out.

"Police! Stop!"

Sudo skids to a halt. My dad, in plain clothes, is holding out his badge and walking toward him. A circle of kids gathers around us. Sudo looks at me, panicked. Like an animal caught in a trap.

"I thought you understood the rules," he hisses. "I thought you were like me."

"I'm not," I say. "It just took me a while to figure that out."

Only a few minutes later, cops are swarming the area. Sudo is in the back of a blue-and-white police cruiser. His black eyes stare out at me until the car drives away.

Chapter Fifteen

The sunlight gleams off the tallest obsidian spire of the castle. A little bugchopper flitters by, on its way to the mechanic. Below us an army of Kraken tanks and spiderbots slowly winds its way down a highway into the distance.

"You don't have to do this," says Jane.

"I think it's stupid," says Griggs. "You're giving up some awesome stuff."

Their warfighters are both perched alongside mine, in the tallest turret of the castle. We watch my army slowly empty out of the fortress and head off into the distance. Soon the mechanic will start taking apart the castle, virtual brick by virtual brick.

"It's the right thing to do," I say. "This game isn't the same anymore. Or maybe I'm different. Anyway, I don't need it the way I used to."

"I guess Sudo isn't going to be using it either."

"Not for a while," I say. "Dad said it's going to take some time for him to get through the courts. He's at some kind of facility until they get things sorted out."

"Huh," says Griggs. His warfighter scans the horizon. "You're right. Tear it down. So, see you later?"

"Yeah," I say. "But not here. At school."

"You got it." Griggs's warfighter
vanishes in a spray of pixels.

Jane and I leap off the turret and land
in a cloud of pixelated dust at the base of
the castle. I key in the final commands
and we watch as the mechanic starts
disassembling the massive structure.
Soon nothing will remain of the castle—
just the sketches in the margins of my
school notebooks.

"What about me? When am I going
to see you next?" asks Jane.

"Soon," I say. "I won't make you
wait around." She cuts her connection.
I take off my headset and close the
laptop lid. Beside it, on my cluttered
desk, is an airplane ticket to Chicago.
Just for a visit. But it's a chance to see
her. In real life.

PREVIEW OF TAP OUT

978-1-4598-0875-1 pb
978-1-4598-0876-8 pdf
978-1-4598-0877-5 epub

Chapter One

Dear Son,

It has been a while since I wrote to you. I am sorry and will not make excuses for that. The last letter you sent to me was about how much you hate your new school. I think that I would hate it too, but your mother thinks it is the best for you. And there is not much I can do from where I am, is there?

So all I can do is give you some good advice. I think it is a father's job to tell you how the world is. Not what it should be. And I tell you that you must fight every single day of your life. Whether with your fists or just the way you live every day, you will have to fight for everything. I know that I have.

And so when you wrote that you hate your new school, that is okay. In fact, I think hate is good.

Because in the end, the winner of any fight is decided by a few small things.

The winner is the one who doesn't crap his pants.

The winner takes fewer punches than the other guy.

And the winner hates just a little bit more. And has enough control to let that hate out, hit by hit.

Dad

Chapter Two

"I don't want any trouble," I say.

It's a lie.

I'm actually kind of hoping the bald guy makes the first move. It's been one of my bad days, where my skin doesn't feel like it fits. Like I'm just waiting for someone to come at me. I'm edgy. Pissed off. Looking for a fight. And I found one—this over-muscled chrome dome shoving around a skinny kid with glasses in front of the convenience store.

The bald guy in the Lakers jersey looks slowly over his shoulder at me and then snorts. He exaggerates letting go of his victim—his fingers snap open to release the kid with glasses. The kid's wearing the same uniform as me. The uniform of Norfolk Academy.

Bald guy swaggers toward me. "What, you standing up for him? Private-school code of honor?" He laughs and shakes his head. "Would be funny, except your friend Jonathan here owes me money. So, you step off and let me finish my business."

"Mason," says the victim—Jonathan—from behind him. "Take it easy, bro. We can sort—"

I stand my ground. "Know what? I don't know him and I don't know you. And I don't care what your business is with him. But you don't do it on the street in front of me."

"Or what? You gonna get your nice white shirt all dirty?" Mason gives me a shove, both hands on my chest. I stumble and then come back fast. Push him with one hand on his Lakers jersey. He doesn't move, but his expression darkens. Game on.

Sean Rodman's interest in writing for teenagers came out of working at schools around the world. In Australia, he taught ancient history to future Olympic athletes. Closer to home, he worked with students from over 100 countries at a nonprofit international school. He is currently the executive director of the Story Studio Writing Society, a charity dedicated to unleashing the creativity of young writers and improving literacy. Sean lives in Victoria, British Columbia. For more information, visit www.srodman.com.

Titles in the Series

orca soundings